TOMMY DONBAVAND'S FUNNY SHORTS

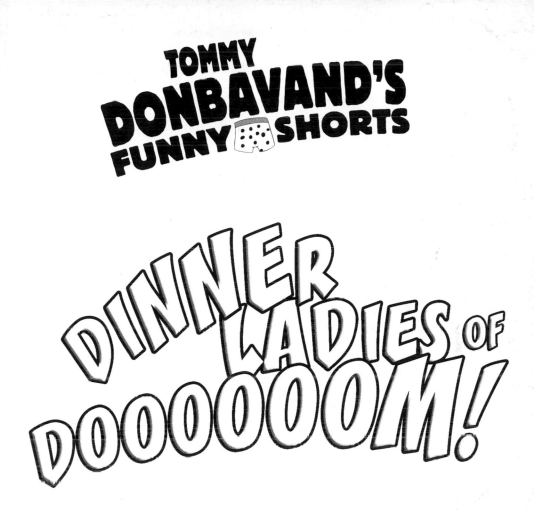

DINNER LADIES OF DOOOOOOM!

WRITTEN BY TOMMY DONBAVAND
ILLUSTRATED BY KEVIN MYERS

EDGE FRANKLIN WATTS

LONDON·SYDNEY

Franklin Watts
First published in Great Britain in 2018 by The Watts Publishing Group

Credits
Executive Editor: Adrian Cole
Design Manager: Peter Scoulding
Cover Designer: Cathryn Gilbert
Illustrations: Kevin Myers

HB ISBN 978 1 4451 5385 8
PB ISBN 978 1 4451 5387 2
Library ebook ISBN 978 1 4451 5386 5

Printed in China.

Franklin Watts
An imprint of
Hachette Children's Group
Part of The Watts Publishing Group
Carmelite House
50 Victoria Embankment
London EC4Y 0DZ

An Hachette UK Company
www.hachette.co.uk

www.franklinwatts.co.uk

Contents

CHAPTER ONE
Friend

Bored!

Bored! Bored! Bored!

Boredboredboredboredboredboredbored!

BOOOOOOOOOOOOOOOOOOOOOOOOORED!

"What are you doing?" hissed a voice.

Cam looked up from his exercise book.

Someone had asked him a question. Please

let it not be Miss McKay ...

"I said, what are you doing?"

Phew! It wasn't Miss McKay. It was his best

mate, Usman, sitting next to him.

Panic over!

"Isn't it obvious?" Cam whispered,

continuing to scribble on the page.

"I'm wasting time."

"By writing the same word over

and over again?"

Cam nodded. "You'd be amazed just how much time this actually wastes."

"You should be paying attention," said Usman. "We're in the middle of maths!"

Cam looked at the clock on the wall. "No, we're near the end of maths. There's just two minutes until lunch. I'll be fine, so long as Miss McKay doesn't ask me a quest—"

"Cameron Green," said Miss McKay. "I have a question for you."

Of course she did.

"Yes, Miss?"

"Please could you tell me the answer to the equation we've just been discussing?"

Uh-oh.

"Are you sure you want me to do it, Miss?"

"Yes, Cameron. You've been writing in your exercise book all morning, so I presume you have the right answer ..."

Someone sighed on the other side of the room. Cam didn't need to look to see who it was. He'd know that sigh anywhere. It was what his twin sister, Holly, did whenever she thought he was being an idiot.

Holly sighed a lot.

"Sometime today, please," said Miss McKay. "I have a staff meeting to get to."

Cam started to panic, and then Usman came to the rescue. He always paid attention in maths. Cam looked across to find his friend mouthing the answer to the problem on the board. Yes! Everything was going to be OK!

Cam carefully studied Usman's lips, then turned confidently back to Miss McKay.

"The answer to the equation is ... Cornwall!"

After class, Holly caught up with Cam just as he reached the doors to the dining hall.

"What was that?"

Cam scowled. "What was what?"

"What was that ridiculous answer for?"

"It was a guess," said Cam with a shrug.

"A guess? You do realise that people know we're twins, don't you? I can't even pretend to have been adopted by a family who already had an idiot for a son!"

Now, it was Cam's turn to sigh. "All right!" he said, pushing open the door to the dining room. "You've made your point, and I'm sure Miss McKay will do the same this afternoon. Now, if you don't mind, I just want some greasy food and a kick about. Doris the dinner lady has promised me a triple-decker beefburger toda— Oh no!"

Cam stopped, a look of horror washing over his face.

Holly followed his gaze. There were two different dinner ladies standing exactly where Doris and Betty should have been. And there was a new menu pinned to the wall. A menu that started with the words: 'All New Vegetarian Lunches', then underneath that, 'No burgers'.

Cam raced to the front of the queue. "Excuse me, where's Doris?"

The thinner of the two new dinner ladies glared at him. "Who?"

"Doris," repeated Cam. "She normally

does your job. Or, maybe her job," he said, pointing to the other unfamiliar figure.

"Oh, that dinner lady," snarled the woman. "She doesn't work here any more, ain't that right, Alison?"

The second dinner lady nodded slowly, her

ball of brown hair bobbing along. "That's right, Pat. She's gone. They both have."

Cam leaned over the counter and spoke in a loud whisper. "Did they leave any beefburgers sizzling on the griddle for me?"

"Ain't no beefburgers here, boy!" Alison snapped. "We don't do meat."

"It says so on the menu," added Pat.

Cam nodded. "Yes, I saw that, but I presumed it was some kind of joke."

Alison snarled. "We never joke about vegetables, boy!"

Holly stepped in before Cam could offend the newcomers further. "I'm sorry, Pat ..."

"It's Miss O'Cake to you!" Pat growled.

"Wait," said Cam. "Your name is Pat ...
O'Cake?"

Pat ran her fingers through her greasy
red hair. "It's Irish!"

"It's lovely!" said Cam, biting down on
his bottom lip. He turned to Pat O'Cake's
workmate. "And you are Alison ..."

"Wonderland!" snapped the larger
dinner lady.

"Alison Wonderland," said Cam, his face
twitching. Holly kicked him in the shin.

"Ow!" he moaned, rubbing his leg.
Both dinner ladies leaned over the
counter, their expressions fierce.

"Now, pick something from the menu,
or go away!"

CHAPTER TWO
Food

Cam poked at the pile of mush on his plate.

"What did you get?" Usman asked.

"I can't tell," Cam admitted. "I think it might be sprout surprise."

"I got that," said Class 3's Abbie Jones from the next table. She gestured to a plate with six sprouts sitting on it. "I'm not sure what the surprise is, though."

"You must have the curry, then..." said Usman. "The lettuce curry."

"What does it taste like?" asked Holly.

Usman reached over with a fork and tried a bit of Cam's lunch. He chewed for a moment, then shook his head. "It doesn't taste of anything," he said, turning back to his cabbage toastie.

"And to think, I *accidentally* left my packed lunch at home for this," said Cam.

Holly reached beneath the table and produced a football-themed lunchbox. "Good job I brought it then, isn't it?"

Cam grabbed the lunchbox and opened it. "If you weren't my sister I'd kiss you ..." he began, then he thought for a moment. "No, I still wouldn't kiss you, even then. Thanks, though."

Cam lifted up one of his sandwiches and sniffed at it. "Ah ... ham!" he breathed happily. "Sooooo much better than that veggie muck!"

"It'f not bad, acfually," said Usman, his mouth full. "Alfough, I do feel sfrange ..."

Cam chuckled. "You've been strange ever since the first—"

Suddenly, Usman jumped up and stood smartly to attention. "That food has truly satisfied me," he announced. "Now, I should like to return to class for extra maths."

Abbie Jones was the next to leap to her feet. "A super idea, fellow pupil. I shall join you!"

"So shall we!" cried at least forty other students, as they all abandoned their lunches. "Hurrah for extra maths!"

Cam and Holly watched in astonishment as almost all the other kids in the dining room marched towards the exit, singing the six times table.

"One six is six, two sixes are twelve, three sixes are eighteen, four sixes are twenty-four!"

By the time they reached seven sixes, they had all left the dining hall, heading back in the direction of their classrooms.

"OK," said Cam. "Maybe it's just me,
but that was officially weird."

Holly looked around the room. The
only pupils left were those eating packed

lunches, and they all looked just as confused as she and Cam did.

"Come on," she said, snapping her lunchbox closed.

Cam stared at her. "You don't want extra maths as well, do you?"

"No! Well, not right now," replied Holly. "I want to find out what's going on ..."

"Let's ask them if they know," said Cam as he noticed the two new dinner ladies heading in their direction.

"Excuse me ..."

Both dinner ladies stopped and tilted their heads slightly, as though listening hard.

"O ... K ..." said Cam, frowning. "Any idea what got into that lot?"

"Yes," said Pat, "we know exactly what has got into them."

"WE have!" finished Alison.

Then, several bizarre things happened all at once. Both dinner ladies grew a pair of tall, metal antennae from the tops of their heads between which bursts of electricity began to buzz and crackle. They each

stretched out their arms, and pointed them towards the children. Finally, a slim, metal tube extended from inside Alison's finger.

Cam and Holly began to back away, keeping their eyes firmly fixed on the weird women.

"Well, thanks for your help. I think that's all the questions we have for now," croaked Cam. "If anything else comes to mind ..."

BLOOP!

Alison's arm jerked and a giant glob of something wet shot out of her metal tube.

The packed-lunch kids started screaming. Cam ducked a blob, and the projectile whizzed over his head. It hit one of the

remaining packed-lunch kids in the face.

SPLAT!

Holly stared. "Is that ... mashed potato?"

The boy nodded as he wiped the goo from
around his mouth. Then, without warning,
he turned and marched towards the doors,
chanting his six times table.

"One six is six, two sixes are twelve …"

BLOOP!

Holly dodged a second lump of mashed potato, this one from Pat. It hit the wall behind her and slid slowly to the floor.

"Come on!" she cried, grabbing her brother's hand.

"Where?" demanded Cam. "Where are we going?"

A third portion of putrid potato shot past them, catching another pupil in the side of the head.

"One six is six, two sixes are twelve …"

"Anywhere but here!" yelled Holly, as the twins burst through the double doors.

CHAPTER THREE
Find

Cam burbled out loud as Holly dragged him along the corridor. "She ... she had ... from her hand ... I saw ... it was ... then, poof! Mashed potato ... I mean, mashed potato!"

Holly pushed open a door, pulled Cam into the room beyond, and slammed it shut. She was busy rifling through a pile of paperwork before Cam realised where they were.

"Whoa! This is Mrs Turner's office!" he exclaimed.

"I know," said Holly, without looking up.

"As in, Mrs Turner — the headteacher!"

"I know, Cam!"

"But what if she catches us?"

"She won't."

"How can you be sure?"

"Because she's in a staff meeting about the school inspector visiting this afternoon."

Cam looked impressed. "How do you know all this stuff?"

"I pay attention in class."

"Rather you than me," said Cam. "And paying attention hasn't told us what's going on around here."

"It must be something to do with the new

dinner ladies," said Holly.

"The dinner ladies said they'd got INTO the kids. What, in the food?" Cam wondered.

"Of course!" said Holly, her eyes wide. "It's OBVIOUS when you think about it."

"It certainly is," agreed Cam. His face slowly twisted into a frown. "Is it?"

"Think about it ..." said Holly. "What are the new dinner ladies?"

"Women?" answered Cam uncertainly. "Wait, are you saying they've put diced women into the school dinners? Eeurgh!"

Holly sighed. Again. "They're not women, Cam. They're robots."

"They are?"

"Electrical antennae, weapons embedded

beneath the flesh, flashing eyes ..."

"Oh, wow!" cried Cam, his eyes wide. "They're robots!"

"Now you're with me!" grinned Holly resuming her search of the desk. "So, if they've put versions of themselves in the food, that must mean ..."

Cam blinked, blank.

This time Holly managed to hold back her sigh long enough to explain. "Nanobots."

"Nanna bots?" said Cam. "Like with grey hair and pockets full of boiled sweets?"

"Nano, not Nanna!" sighed Holly. "As in tiny, microscopic robots. They must be controlling anyone who's eaten them, making them ask for extra schoolwork."

"But that's ... that's horrible!"

"Which is why we've got to put a stop to it," said Holly. "Help me search the office."

"OK," said Cam, pulling open the top drawer of the headteacher's filing cabinet. "What are we looking for?"

Holly shrugged. "Anything that can prove

Mrs Turner is in on all this."

"You really think she is?"

Before his sister could reply, another voice said, "Yes, Holly, you really think I am?"

The twins spun to find Mrs Turner standing in the doorway to the office.

Cam slowly eased the filing cabinet drawer closed. "Hello, miss!" he said as cheerfully as he could under the circumstances. "Holly and I were just looking for you ..."

"I wasn't," said Holly, flatly. "I was looking for evidence that you've replaced our dinner ladies with androids and are controlling pupils with nano-technology."

"Hahahaha!" said Cam, far too loudly. "She's funny, isn't she, miss? Good joke, Holly!"

"It's not a joke," Holly insisted.

"Your sister's quite right, Cameron," said

Mrs Turner, crossing the room to sit on the edge of her desk. "This is all really very serious. Did you find anything?"

Cam started to say 'no', but Holly spoke over him. "Actually, yes I did." She held up two booklets with circuit diagrams on their covers.

"What are they?" asked Cam.

"User manuals," said Holly. "User manuals for robots."

"Android Sapiens Model A113, to be exact," said Mrs Turner. "Although I doubt that your sister, clever as she is, will be able to understand them."

"I can try!" said Holly.

"No, you can't," said Mrs Turner. She snatched the paperwork from Holly's hands, and pressed a button on her desk.

A moment later, the door crashed open, and the two robotic dinner ladies stepped into the room.

"Put them with the others," ordered Mrs Turner. "I'm going to get changed, ready for the inspector."

Pat and Alison crossed the room and grabbed the children tightly by the arms.

"This way!"

Cam and Holly were escorted from the office and back along the corridor — where they were delighted to see their teacher walking towards them.

"Miss McKay!" yelled Cam. "You have to help us!"

But the teacher didn't look at them. She marched straight past, chanting the six times table.

"Six sixes are thirty-six, seven sixes are ..."

They reached the caretaker's supply closet. Alison extended a long piece of metal from the end of her finger, and used it to pick the lock. Then, the androids tossed the twins inside, and slammed the door shut.

Cam tried the handle, but the door didn't budge.

"How are we going to get out of here?" he demanded.

"That's exactly what we've been wondering," said a voice from the shadows.

CHAPTER FOUR
Free

Cam grabbed one of the caretaker's mops and spun round, wielding it like some kind of ninja weapon. Or, that was the plan — until he slapped himself in the face with the wet end.

"Oh, yuck!" he moaned. "Floor water!"

Ignoring him, Holly pushed aside a stack of toilet paper to discover two women in white aprons, tied up at the back of the closet. "Doris!" she cried. "Betty!"

"Our real dinner ladies! I was worried about you two," said Cam.

"That's very kind, Cameron," said Doris, as Holly began to untie her.

"Don't mention it," said Cam. "Now, about the burgers you promised me ..."

"Not now, Cam!" barked Holly.

"But, I'm hungry!"

"We all are," Holly replied.

"Us, too," said Betty. "We've been locked in here since the end of school yesterday."

"It was those rotten robotic replacements!" said Doris with a scowl. "Mrs Turner ordered them to put us somewhere secure."

"Don't worry about them," grinned Holly. "I've got a plan!" With that, she produced a paper booklet with a circuit diagram printed on the front.

Cam gasped. "That's one of the robot's user manuals!"

Holly nodded. "Yep. I managed to hide it up my T-shirt when Mrs Turner caught us."

"But, you gave them to her ..." said Cam.

"I gave her one of them," Holly explained. "The rest were just blank sheets of paper from her printer tray."

"So, what's the plan?" asked Cam.

"Well, first off we need to get out of here. Then, we need to find a robo dinner lady."

Cam stared at his sister for a moment. "I thought we wanted to avoid the dinner ladies of doooooom?"

"Why did you say 'doom' like that?"

"Because two 'o's aren't enough to express quite how horrible they are," said Cam. "The word needs at least six of them."

"I like that!" said Doris, rubbing at the red marks where the rope had dug into her wrists. "Let's go and stop the dinner ladies of doooooom!"

All four captives shared a high five, then turned to face the locked cupboard door.

"Erm, so how do you plan to get out of here exactly?" asked Betty.

"Hello? Is there anybody here?"

Mr Oliver F. Stead, school inspector, stood in the entrance of Penny Vale School and tapped the bell on the counter three more times. He wasn't at all impressed with the lack of reception — something he generally got when visiting a school. He clicked the top of his pen and made a comment in his notebook to reflect these feelings.

"No-one to greet me on arrival. Minus ten points."

He was just about to turn and leave, when Mrs Turner appeared, out of breath and red in the face. She opened the security door and ushered the inspector inside.

"Mr ... Stead!" she said between gasps. "My ... apologies for ... keeping ... you waiting."

The inspector clicked his pen again and made another note: "Headteacher out of breath and unable to converse without extended pauses. Minus six points."

Mrs Turner looked horrified. "What? Surely you don't have to do that ..."

CLICK!

"Questioning actions of school inspector. Minus twelve points."

The headteacher fixed her expression into a cheesy grin. "Well done. Yes. I deserved that. Now, would you care to look around, or do you want a cup of tea first?"

Mr Stead studied the headteacher through narrowed eyes, his thumb hovering over the top of his pen.

Mrs Turner looked nervously from the inspector, to his pen, and back again.

"A cup of tea would be very welcome, thank you."

"Oh, good!" said Mrs Turner. "If you would be kind enough to follow me ..."

The headteacher led the way down the corridor. The inspector followed, running his fingertips over the walls and checking them for dust.

They had just passed the caretaker's cupboard when the door eased open and four pairs of eyes peered out from the darkness beyond.

"Well done!" hissed Betty. "Taking the lock apart worked, after all!"

"I knew it would," said Holly, returning a metal nail file to Doris. "Keep that handy in case we need a screwdriver again."

Doris nodded. "Is anyone out there?"

"Mrs Turner," whispered Betty. "She's with a man — it's probably the school inspector."

"We need to tell him what's going on!" urged Cam.

"Not yet," said Doris. "We have to deal with those tin tyrants first."

"Right," said Holly. "It looks clear. Come on, let's go!"

The four of them stepped out into the corridor — just as Pat O'Cake stomped around the corner, her antennae sparking brightly.

"Halt!" she commanded, aiming her mashed-potato blaster in their direction. "One false move, and I'll splat you with sloppy spuds!"

CHAPTER FIVE
Fzzzt!

Cam, Holly and the two dinner ladies were pushed into the dining room by Pat.

"Now, we will make you like everybody else!" said Pat, sparks of electricity fizzing between her metal antennae.

Cam shivered. "You mean ... we'll love maths!"

Pat gave a robotic nod. "Not just maths! You'll adore poetry, dream about spellings, and beg for history lessons."

"NO!" cried Cam. "I just want to play football!" Suddenly, he kicked his lunchbox from where he had left it earlier. It spun in the air for a few seconds then, as it began to fall, Cam struck it on the volley.

The plastic projectile shot across the room and wedged itself between Pat's two metallic aerials, blocking the flow of electricity between them. There was a

FZZZT! sound, then the dreadful dinner lady's eyes crossed and she fell to the floor with a CLANG!

"Quick," said Cam, "fix her before she has chance to reboot."

Betty tore open the back of Pat's shirt, revealing a dull silver torso beneath. Using the tip of her nail file, Doris began to unscrew the flap on the android's back.

"This looks simple enough," said Holly. She scanned the programming instructions in the user manual. "We need to key in a couple of tricky maths equations."

"I'll leave that bit to you," said Cam with a wink.

Out in the main corridor, Mr O. F. Stead stood and stared. He had been expecting the school's pupils to be hard at work in class but, instead, they had formed two long lines down the sides of the corridor.

CLICK!

"Students in unusual location. Minus fifty-two points."

"No, it's fine," said Mrs Turner from behind the inspector. "They've only come out of class to do something special for you."

Mr Stead scowled.

CLICK!

"Taking an inspector by surprise. Minus thir—"

Before he could say more, the girl on his right proclaimed: "E equals MC squared!"

The inspector blinked, surprised. "Y-yes, that's correct. Einstein's theory—"

Then Usman, next in line, spoke up: "The square of the hypotenuse is equal to the sum of the squares of the other two sides!"

"Again, that is absolutely—"

It was now the turn of the next pupil on the right: "The area of a circle is Pi times the radius, squared."

To the left: "Pi, rounded to the tenth decimal place is 3.1415926536."

Right: "The diameter of the Earth is 12,742 kilometres."

"The Sun generates energy by fusing hydrogen nuclei into helium."

"That's 620 million metric tons of hydrogen every second."

"The capital city of Peru is Lima."

"AC electric current was invented by Nikola Tesla."

The pupils continued to announce what they knew, one by one, all along the corridor.

By now, Mr Stead was clicking the button on his pen so fast, it sounded like he was rapping in morse code. He began to skip happily on the spot.

"Yes, yes, yes!" he cried, tears streaming down his cheeks. "Causing a school inspector to experience utter happiness. Plus five thousand — no, plus ten thousand points!"

He spun to face Mrs Turner. "Please," he begged, "tell me how you do it."

"It's all down to these dinner ladies," said a voice.

The headteacher and inspector turned to find Cam and Holly approaching with Pat O'Cake and Alison Wonderland behind them.

"They did all this?" said Mr Stead.

Cam nodded. "Well, it was the nanobots

they fed to the pupils. Would you like to see what this school is really like, without all the brain meddling."

"What?" spat Mrs Turner. "You wouldn't dare ..."

"Oh," said Holly with a smile, "we would dare! Pat, Alison?"

The two dinner ladies of doooooom opened their mouths and yelled, "Nanobots, return!"

"Heurgh!"

"Bluuurgh!"

"Mmmppphhh!"

"Oh, no!" said Mrs Turner.

"Oh, yes," said Cam with a grin. "You see, to recall the nanobots, I'm afraid the food they were added to will have to make a comeback as well ..."

Mr Stead stared in horror as dozens of

pupils began to vomit at the same time.

"No!" screamed Mrs Turner, racing down the corridor, trying to force the pupils to clamp their hands over their mouths — but to no avail. She got part way down and slipped in a puddle of puke. Just as she stood up in the swelling, stinking sea of sick, she threw up over Mr O. F. Stead.

And made Mr Stead sick.

CLICK!

"Causing ... hlurrf! A school inspect ...

hrrrriimmm! To blow chunks. Minus one

million points! Huurreeugh!"

"Yuck!" said Holly, as countless

microscopic nanobots left their hosts

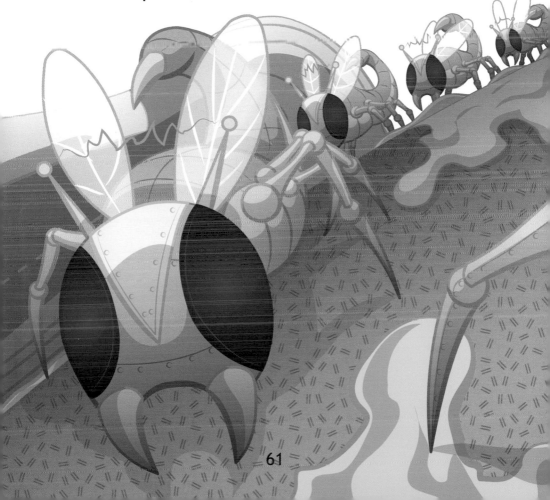

and flew back to the two robots.

"This is disgusting."

  "And yet, I'm still hungry," said Cam. "Let's go back to the dining room. Doris promised me she's got a cheeseburger with my name on it!"